Nasty
STORIES for
Good boys and girls

CHRISTOPHER·MILNE

That Dirty Dog
and Other Naughty Stories for Good Boys and Girls
published in 2011 by
Hardie Grant Egmont
85 High Street
Prahran, Victoria 3181, Australia
www.hardiegrantegmont.com.au

PEFC
PEFC/21-31-16

The pages of this book are printed on paper derived
from forests promoting sustainable management.

A CiP record for this title is available from the National Library of Australia

Text copyright © 2011 Christopher Milne
Illustration and design copyright © 2011 Hardie Grant Egmont

Illustration and design by Simon Swingler
Typesetting by Ektavo
Printed in Australia

1 3 5 7 9 10 8 6 4 2

Other books by Christopher Milne
The Day Our Teacher Went Mad and Other Naughty Stories
The Bravest Kid I've Ever Known and Other Naughty Stories
The Girl Who Blew Up Her Brother and Other Naughty Stories
An Upside-Down Boy and Other Naughty Stories
The Girl With Death Breath and Other Naughty Stories
The Crazy Dentist and Other Naughty Stories
The Toilet Rat of Terror and Other Naughty Stories

Also available from www.christophermilne.com.au
The Western Sydney Kid
Little Johnnie and the Naughty Boat People

that
dirty
dog

-AND-
OTHER

Naughty
STORIES FOR
Good boys and girls

CHRISTOPHER MILNE

Illustrations by
Simon Swingler

hardie grant EGMONT

TO PETE AND ROB

Peter and Robert are my two sons and they provided the inspiration for most of my stories. They have always been a bit naughty in real life, but also brave, clever, decent and funny — and much-loved.

Pete and Rob went to Nayook Primary School and many of these stories are loosely based on those wonderful years.

Christopher McTier

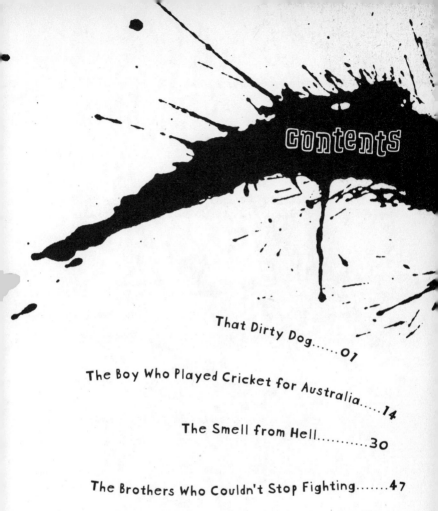

Contents

that dirty dog

My dad's tough. **Really tough**. He drives a big Mack truck and he reckons he's never cried in his life.

For breakfast, he has cornflakes, but always in a dirty bowl. And if he's got a lot of heavy lifting to do that day, he sprinkles

My dad

crushed bricks on top. Or that's what he tells me, anyway – I'm usually asleep when he leaves.

Except for Saturdays. Dad starts late on Saturdays and if I've been good, he lets me come with him on his trip to the brickworks. We always go along exactly the same road and each time we pass the park, we see a dog. The same dog, in exactly the same spot.

'There's that stupid dog again,' said Dad one day. 'What a useless, dirty-looking mutt. What a scumbag.'

'Looks a bit hungry,' I said.

'So what?' said Dad. 'Should get off its lazy butt and rip into a couple of rubbish bins.'

I wouldn't have minded stopping to give it a cuddle, but I'd never say so, of course. Dad would call me a wuss. A big sooky-baby.

Dad reckoned everyone was a wuss. Unless they drove a truck and drank beer like him.

The next Saturday, that poor, dirty old dog was there again, with its big sad eyes, looking as hungry as any dog I'd ever seen.

'What a filth bag!' yelled Dad. 'What a loser. Pity someone hasn't run it over.'

I didn't say anything. Sometimes I didn't like my dad very much.

And so it was. Every Saturday, Jack — that's what I decided to call him — would be sitting there, almost like he was waiting for

us to come. Until one day, when he wasn't there at all.

I looked everywhere, my face pressed up against the window, but I found nothing.

'Wonder where he is?' I said as we kept driving.

'Who cares?' said Dad. 'The mutt's better off dead, anyway.'

On the way back past the park that day, I asked, 'Couldn't I have a quick look?'

'For that rotten mongrel?' asked Dad. 'You've got to be joking.'

'Please, Dad,' I said. 'He might be lying hurt somewhere. I'll clean the truck for you. All of it. I promise! Inside, too.'

Now, it so happened that Dad's footy team was playing on TV that night, and he knew that if he washed the truck himself he'd miss the first half.

'Oh, all right,' he said. 'Make it quick or I'll leave you here.'

Sure enough, Jack was hurt. Badly. Hit by a car, probably. I found him lying behind a tree, bleeding from the mouth.

'Dad!' I screamed. 'You've got to help me. Jack's been hurt!'

'Leave the useless thing to die,' yelled Dad.

I leant down to cuddle poor Jack and he tried to lick me. But he was too sore to move.

I started to cry.

'Hell's bells!' grumbled Dad. He'd come over to have a look by now. 'If there's one thing I can't stand, it's a bloke crying. Get out of the way and give me a look.'

Dad felt around Jack's tummy and said, 'Yep, he's hurt all right. So now what?'

I just looked up at Dad, trying not to cry again.

Dad sighed, shook his head and said, 'All right. Anything to stop your blubbering.' And with that, Dad picked Jack up and put him in the back of the truck. 'I'll drop him at the vet, but if it's going to cost anything to fix him, we'll have to put him down.'

'Put him down?' I asked.

'Yep. Knock him off. Put him to sleep. He's probably going to cark it anyway.'

Sure enough, the vet said Jack looked really bad. But he couldn't be sure how bad until he'd taken an X-ray.

As the vet carried him out, Jack looked up and his big sad eyes said, 'I understand if you decide not to help me. Who'd want an old dog like me anyway?'

Dad and I sat in the waiting room in silence. My mouth was dry and I had a sick feeling in my stomach. It would have helped so much if Dad had said something nice about Jack, or how sorry he felt for him, but instead

he just stared at the wall.

At last the vet came back.

I could tell straight away from the look on the vet's face that the news was bad. Broken ribs, and three hundred and sixty dollars to fix him.

'Right,' said Dad, 'that's all I need to know. You can put him down. Sooner the better, I say.'

'No!' I sobbed. 'I'll pay, somehow. Please, Dad!'

Dad just shook his head. Suddenly, something inside me went funny. Something I'd never felt before.

'I hate you!' I shouted. 'You reckon

9

everyone else is a wuss, but you know what? I think you are. Because you're too scared to do something nice!' And with that I turned and ran.

I'd never spoken to my dad like that before, and I expected him to chase me down and ground me for a year. But he didn't.

When he came out of the vet's a few minutes later, I saw him wipe his eye with his sleeve.

'Got some of that dog dirt in my eye,' he muttered.

On the way home, neither of us said anything. Nothing.

That night, no-one said much either.

Except for Mum, who asked Dad when his fishing trip was coming up this year.

'Might not go,' said Dad.

'But you love it,' said Mum.

'Gets a bit boring,' said Dad. 'Anyway, we could use the money.'

'What for?' asked Mum. Dad didn't answer.

I didn't even mention Jack after that. I'd told Dad I hated him for putting Jack down. What else was there to say?

Not that I didn't think about poor Jack. I thought about nothing else. I reckon it's the saddest I've ever felt.

It was about a week later that Dad came home and said, 'I've got something to show you.'

I guessed he had a new truck, so I walked outside for a look. And there, sitting in the front seat of Dad's old Mack, was the nicest thing I've ever seen.

Jack, with his fur all washed, his tail wagging and a great big bandage around his tummy.

I raced over and gave Jack the most massive hug of his life. Then I turned and said, 'I love you, Dad.'

'And I love you too,' said Dad. This time, he must have had dirt in both eyes.

Jack goes everywhere with Dad now. When Dad does a job picking up sheep or cows, Jack helps round them up.

'So he should,' says Dad. 'Rotten mongrel owes me heaps.'

In the morning, Dad leans down and lets Jack lick his face. If that's tough, I want to be just like my dad.

the boy who played cricket for Australia

Peter Wallace was mad about cricket. 'Cricket-crazy,' his dad said.

It was cricket-this, cricket-that. Cricket before school. Cricket after school. If Pete didn't have a bat or ball in his hand, his mum used to take his temperature.

Peter wouldn't let his dad or his little brother Robbie rest for a minute. Always wanting to have a hit in the backyard, always wanting to bat first, and never, ever going out LBW. Some nights Peter wore his pads to bed. And Rob reckoned that on windy, scary nights, he wore his protector as well.

As Peter grew older, he started to play in the under-thirteens competition. His love of cricket became even greater. And people started noticing something. Peter was becoming a good little player.

But Pete didn't want to be just good. He wanted to play for Australia! It was something he'd heard on the radio that did it. A young

Indian batsman was asked when he'd first wanted to play for India. 'From the moment I picked up a bat,' he answered.

Yes, that's me! Pete thought. *I'm not crazy. I want to play for my country too!*

Pete's dad said there was nothing wrong with aiming for the top, but that he shouldn't forget cricket was just a game. 'Play for fun and try your best,' he said. 'And everything else will take care of itself.'

Sounds pretty wussy to me, thought Pete, but he just said, 'Yes, Dad.'

Pete's dad was always coming out with mushy stuff. *Must have been a bit of a loser when he was young*, thought Pete. *If you want to play*

for Australia, you've got to go for it!

And then it happened. The most fantastic, unbelievable day of days.

Pete had gone into a muesli bar cricket competition. **And won!** The prize was the first day at a test match with Australia playing against England. But the best part was a chance to go to the Australian team breakfast and then down to the change rooms before the game. Pete would get all the players' autographs and watch them warm up and stuff.

Pete was so excited that he thought he might have kittens.

The game was at the most famous place in the world, the Melbourne Cricket Ground,

and the newspapers said it would be packed. And so it was. Luckily Pete had arrived early.

After waiting in a queue for what seemed like half of Pete's life, he and his family finally reached the entrance to the Members' Stand. Pete was dressed in his whites, carrying his bat in one hand and his muesli bar prize letter in the other.

The man at the gate said, 'We've been expecting you. Didn't someone mention that you didn't need to queue up? You could have come straight in. Unfortunately you're a bit late for the breakfast, but I'm sure you'll be well looked after.'

On the other side of the gate were two

men – one to take Pete's family to their seats in the stand, the other to take Pete through to meet the players.

Suddenly, there Pete was. Surrounded by the most important, fantastic, excellent people ever. The Australian cricket team. Ricky Ponting, Michael Clarke – they were all there. And Pete was introduced to every one of them. He was in heaven.

Then Mr Ponting asked if Pete would like to stay with the team once the game had started. You can probably guess what Pete's answer was.

'Yes!'

Well, the game had been going for an hour and Australia had started terribly. Three wickets down for only fifteen runs!

But the real disaster had only just begun. Something even worse was happening in the change rooms. Something only Pete knew about.

The next batsman, Michael Clarke, who was supposed to be padding up, was instead being terribly sick in the toilets. It must have been something he'd eaten for breakfast.

Pete was trying to help by giving him wet towels and lemonade, but the batsman just got worse.

'What are you going to do?' asked Pete

from outside the toilet door.

'I don't know,' croaked Clarkey (that's what Pete calls him now that he knows him personally). 'Do you think you could run up and tell Punter for me? He's in the players' room at the top of the stairs.'

'Sure,' said Pete.

'And Pete,' said Clarkey, 'you've been a terrific help. Thanks. Maybe I can give you a hand one day when you play for Australia?'

Pete smiled and ran off. And then he stopped.

Those words, Play for Australia...

And Pete started to think of something very, very naughty.

Pete's family were sitting in the grandstand and they groaned with the rest of the crowd as yet another wicket fell.

Pete's mum was the first to notice the new player marching out to bat. 'Oh, no!' she said.

'It couldn't be!' said his dad.

It was.

Peter Wallace **was marching out to bat.**

Mr Ponting waved madly and shouted at Pete to come back, but Pete kept walking.

The crowd couldn't believe it. 'Who is he?' they asked each other.

'How could someone so short be sent out to bat?'

'Why wasn't the team change in this morning's papers?'

It was all too late. Pete was at the crease. And Stuart Broad was charging in to bowl.

The first three balls whistled past somewhere near Pete's nose. He knew that because he heard them. So he was pleased that he at least saw the fourth ball go past.

But the fifth, that was the ball he was going to get. Pete had decided he would have a whack at it no matter what.

'Cop this, Stuey-baby,' said Pete, and **bang!** The ball rocketed off Pete's bat, over the top of slips, and into the fence for four.

The crowd went wild. But the sixth ball thundered into Pete's pads.

'How's that!' screamed the English team. **'Not out,'** said Pete. He was so used to umpiring at home that the words just popped out.

The umpire got such a shock that he didn't say anything.

And that was the end of the over. Unfortunately, it was also the end of Pete. The police had found him out by now and

Pete was asked to leave the ground.

'Can I stay a bit longer?' Pete asked. Now that he had Broad beaten, he was ready to really cut loose! The policeman shook his head.

So, Pete turned, thanked everyone for coming and proudly marched off the ground. The crowd cheered wildly and Pete lifted his bat in the air, like great batsmen do. Just because his magnificent innings had been cut short, that was no reason to disappoint the crowd.

But that wasn't the end of it. England suddenly realised they could force Australia to make Pete bat again in the second innings,

because you're not allowed to change the team halfway through the game. It was as if Australia now only had ten men in their side, or so they thought.

And so it came to this. After five fantastic days of cricket, Pete – who had, of course, been held back until last in the hope that he wouldn't have to bat again – was suddenly the last man, or boy, standing. Australia had made up a lot of ground, but they were still nine wickets down. They needed three runs to win!

'Don't worry, Mr Ponting,' said Pete. 'I'm young, but I'm still an Aussie!'

As Pete marched out to bat again, he

lifted his bat to thank the crowd, who by now were making a **thunderous roar.**

As Pete took block and looked around the field, the crowd fell silent. Everyone was sick with nerves. Stuart Broad charged in, raised himself up to maximum height and hurled down an absolutely wicked ball that was probably his fastest of the day.

Now, when you've played cricket with your brother in the backyard, day after day, usually until it's too dark to see, you get a sixth sense. You don't even need to see the ball, you just know where it is. And so it was with Pete.

He took a step forward, swung truly,

and sweetly cracked a brilliant cover-drive straight to the fence.

They say the roar from the crowd was heard in London.

the smell from Hell

Janet Wong and Maria Gallus were chatting away one lunchtime when a terrible smell surrounded them.

'Was that you?' asked Janet.

'No!' replied Maria.

'Have I stood in something?' asked Janet,

checking the soles of her shoes.

'Don't think so,' said Maria. 'Maybe it's my lunchbox. Mum's probably given me egg sandwiches again.'

But that wasn't it either. Janet and Maria couldn't work it out. They checked to see if there was a drain nearby, and then each other's breath – even their armpits and sneakers. Nothing!

The smell was getting worse. Other kids were looking around too. Everyone started holding their noses.

Then things became serious. One boy fainted and others started retching.

The smell was absolutely revolting. Think

broken sewer pipes, mixed with garlic breath, mixed with rotten-egg gas, mixed with socks that have been worn for seven days in a row.

Suddenly it all became clear. Standing nearby, wearing a huge grin, was Stinky Adams.

Stinky had only arrived the day before, with a whole lot of other kids whose school was damaged by fire. Rumours had gone around about Stinky, though no-one really believed his smells could be that bad.

But now everyone knew. Stinky Adams did smells that were **sick-making**.

The trouble was that Stinky enjoyed doing smells. It gave him a feeling of power,

and relief, of course. It made him smile. If Stinky found himself surrounded by people choking and kids throwing up, it was a good day.

Of course, Mrs Hammond, the school principal, was not happy. She called Stinky into her office.

'I'm not quite sure how to put this,' said Mrs Hammond, 'but it's come to my attention that you have a small problem downstairs.'

Stinky didn't understand.

'A problem with wind,' continued Mrs Hammond. 'In fact, if I'm to believe the stories, your wind is bordering on scary. "Like a punch in the face" is how one of our

teachers described it. It has to stop. Diet can be a big help. Tell me what you had for breakfast this morning.'

'Mum says I need building up, so she's been giving me big breakfasts,' replied Stinky. 'Today I had stewed prunes, then leftover cauliflower cheese and cabbage fried like hash browns, two eggs, bacon, two pork sausages, a whole can of baked beans…'

'Enough, enough!' said Mrs Hammond.

'Oh, no,' said Stinky.

'What?' asked Mrs Hammond.

'Talking about food like that gets me excited. I think I've just done another smell,' said Stinky.

Now, smelling a fluff out in the open is one thing, but trying to get away from it in a small space like a principal's office is another.

Mrs Hammond didn't even make it to the door. The last thing she remembered was being hit by a stench that was almost too bad to describe.

'Try to imagine,' she said later to the ambulance officer, 'opening the back doors of a truck that has been sitting in the hot sun for two weeks – and finding a dead elephant inside.'

Mrs Hammond was only away for a week, but in that time the school really changed. And all because of Stinky. Kids

were organised to track his movements during lunchtime so they could warn others to steer clear of him and, just like fire drills, teachers taught everyone how to leave the building quickly and safely if Stinky let one go inside.

Mrs Hammond didn't dare call Stinky into her office for another chat – one brush with death was enough – so, until Stinky's old school was rebuilt, they would just have to put up with him. Kids began wearing coats inside because the windows were always open, and some even had gas masks that their parents had bought for them.

Then one day, Mrs Hammond got some

even worse news. The government had decided to test every kid in the country so that they could work out which were the best and worst schools.

Mrs Hammond was immediately against the idea because it was so unfair. Schools in some areas might have a lot of kids whose parents worked long hours to put food on the table, which might mean they didn't have much time to help their kids with schoolwork and reading and stuff. And other parents might be in trouble or going through a really hard time. So when the test results came through, that school would get a bad rating – even if the teachers were

doing a fantastic job helping those kids to keep up. Which made it a good school!

'So,' said Mrs Hammond to her teachers, 'our school is not going to take part in this test because it's wrong.'

'But the government will insist,' said Mr Brown, one of the teachers. 'Won't you be putting your job at risk?'

'I don't care,' said Mrs Hammond.

'There might be another way,' said Mr Brown, looking slightly nervous. 'But it's disgusting.'

Well, Mr Brown's idea was worse than disgusting. But Mrs Hammond agreed to it. She had no choice.

Mr Brown's plan was this: the government would definitely send someone along to supervise the test, to make sure things were done properly and no-one cheated. 'But,' he said, 'what if the supervisor couldn't stay in the room?'

'And how might that come about?' asked Mrs Hammond.

'Stinky Adams,' replied Mr Brown.

Mr Brown needed the kids' help for this plan, and he explained to them that Mrs Hammond thought the test was unfair. It would be tough, he said, but the plan was for Stinky to let one go during the test so that the supervisor was forced to leave the room.

But! The kids would have to pretend that nothing had happened. If the supervisor smelt a rat, the trick wouldn't work.

The supervisor could never say that she left because of a terrible smell – that would just sound too rude. So, with a bit of luck, the school's test results wouldn't make it on to the list.

Of course, the big question was how to get the kids to stay in the room during one of Stinky's smells.

'Practice is the answer,' said Mr Brown. 'We can become immune. Every day for the next month, I'm going to ask Stinky to do a really bad smell – I can't believe I'm saying

this – and I'm going to ask you all to last a minute longer than the day before. I'm sure we can do it, but I should warn you. On the day of the test I'm going to ask Stinky to do one of his worst – something truly frightening.'

'Oh, no!' the kids said to each other, gagging already. But they liked Mr Brown and Mrs Hammond, and they were determined to help.

So, the very next day, the practice sessions began. At first, most kids could only last a few seconds before collapsing and gasping for air. But Mr Brown was right. Slowly but surely they got to the stage where they could

last a full thirty minutes, which was probably the length of the test.

Finally, the day arrived. Luckily it was on Stinky's birthday and Mr Brown suggested that he ask his mum for a special breakfast. Two bowls of prunes, four eggs, two bits of bacon, three thick pork sausages, three fried potato cakes and four bits of toast with a really thick layer of peanut butter. That would do the trick.

It certainly did. As the kids sat down to do the test and the supervisor took her place at the front, everyone could tell that Stinky was just about bursting. Stinky looked over to Mr Brown, who nodded. Then, silent but

deadly, **Stinky let it rip.**

Now we've all come across the odd bad smell but this was something else. Something evil and twisted. A very sick puppy. Nothing could help you imagine what it was like – not even the smell of a thousand dead rats, or a hole-in-the-ground dunny, or the breath of someone who had just smoked a hundred cigarettes after not cleaning their teeth for a year, or rotting fish-heads in a bin.

Kids shifted in their seats, held their breath or tried to think of something else – anything except getting up and leaving.

The supervisor's eyes widened as the horrible smell wafted over. What was that

foul stench? And how come no-one else seemed to notice it? Was it her imagination?

Beads of perspiration began to form on her brow and she went white. She held a handkerchief to her mouth and staggered to her feet. She realised she hadn't taken a breath for well over a minute and panic set in. Lurching all over the place, she zig-zagged towards the door.

Kids were twitching in their seats, desperate for her to leave. But there was one more surprise in store. As the supervisor got closer to the door, she got closer to Stinky.

Now, I've seen some huge vomits before,

but this one was a ten. All over the blackboard, all over the floor and even on the ceiling. Finally, the poor supervisor crawled out the door on her hands and knees, and stumbled towards her car in the parking lot.

You could hear the sigh of relief from all the kids. At last, they could leave too!

But it wasn't just a *sigh* everyone had heard. Stinky had let another one go!

the brothers who couldn't stop fighting

Brian and Keith Taylor used to fight like no other brothers before them. They fought from the moment they woke up until last thing at night, when their poor parents would drag them apart and force them to bed. Even then, Brian would still sometimes sneak into

Keith's room for one last punch, or maybe to pull his pillow away or rip his blankets off.

Why they fought so much, their parents could never work out. If Keith had a mate around to stay, Brian would crack the nasties and try to spoil their fun. Perhaps by throwing golf balls at Keith's head. Or pushing him. Or punching him. Or changing the TV to another channel. Or wrecking the cubby-house they'd just spent hours building. Or insisting that whatever they were playing with was his and that he needed it right now!

And the same when Brian had a mate. One day, Brian was mucking around with his friend Steven when they decided to play bockers.

That's when you take it in turns to punch each other on the arm. As hard as you can. The first one to say he can't take it anymore is the loser. It's terrific fun. Especially when the other kid gets tears in his eyes.

Anyway, with each punch, Brian was saying to Steven, 'Is that the best you can do?' Or, 'That didn't hurt.' Suddenly, Keith appeared with a cricket bat and, as hard as he could, went **bang**, right on Brian's shoulder.

'I bet that hurt,' said Keith.

Brian and Keith's fighting drove their parents mad, but never more so than when they started in the car. Sometimes their mother would lean over to give them a smack

but they would flatten themselves against the back seat.

'For the life of me, I'll stop the car and leave you here!' their father would scream.

'It's not my fault,' Keith would yell. 'Brian hit me.'

'Bull,' Brian would shout. 'He had his leg over my side!'

And so it would go.

One night, when the boys were being unusually quiet, their father put his arm around both their shoulders and said, 'When you boys stop fighting for a minute, like now, it makes me and your mum so happy. Doesn't it feel nice? Have you ever realised

that deep down you might actually like each other?'

Brian and Keith looked at each other and for the first time in ages they agreed on something.

'Dad, you're weird,' said Brian.

'A real sicko,' added Keith.

And off they went to their room for a really good fight.

Strange as it might sound, Brian and Keith really did like fighting and in a few short years they found themselves grown up and fighting again. This time, in a war! You see, Brian and Keith had seen ads on TV for the army and straight away both had

thought, *Yes! This is the life for me.*

Like many other brave Australians, they were soon sent overseas to a country where they were fighting to keep the local people safe.

Then came a terrible day. The officer in charge said that ten men were needed to sneak into an enemy weapons supply and blow it up. It would be dangerous – very dangerous – but it was their only hope.

Spies had found out that the enemy had three times as many weapons, and unless the Aussies could take some of them out with a

surprise attack, there'd be trouble.

'Any volunteers?' asked the officer in charge. 'Anyone want to put their hand up?'

Straight away, Brian shouted, 'Yep, count me in.'

'Me too,' said Keith. 'Hate for Brian to get shot and not be there to see it.'

That night, just before they set out, loaded up with bombs, the officer in charge said there was one order that they must stick to no matter what. If someone got shot, the rest were to leave him there to die. That might sound shocking, but there was just no way a single man could be wasted trying to help another.

'Is that clear?' he thundered.

'Yes, sir,' they replied.

Brian and Keith might never have said so, but they were scared. Scared of dying, scared of even thinking about the possibility that they might never see their mum or dad or Australia again.

Well, they had spread out over several hundred metres when a shot went **crack** in the night and Keith went down. Without having even seen the enemy weapons supply, Keith had copped a sniper's bullet right in the stomach.

Although panic gripped him, he lay silent. He wanted to scream out from the pain but

he knew what the rules were. So, as the other men moved forward, knowing they couldn't stop to help, Keith looked down and saw blood, everywhere. Unable to move, he knew that he would bleed to death.

As Keith lay there in the dark, he thought about his family. Particularly about Brian. He loved his brother so much, but he realised he'd never said so. Just like their dad had said.

Suddenly, a hand. A hand was pulling at his shirt. Pulling him up. Was he imagining it? No. It was a hand that he knew. A hand that had wrestled and held him down and punched him a thousand times.

It was Brian hauling him up and over his shoulder, and saying softly, 'Didn't think I'd leave you, did you?'

'But the orders,' Keith managed to whisper.

'Guess they forgot we're brothers,' said Brian. 'Hang on tight, keep your head down and your mouth shut. Get any blood on me and you're dead.'

As Brian crawled across the ground with Keith clinging desperately to his back, bullets whizzing above their heads, Keith whispered, 'There's something I've got to tell you. My guts are bad, Brian. Really bad. In case I don't make it, you know I've always loved you, don't you?'

'Not going to cry on me as well, are you?' replied Brian. 'Anyway, you are going to make it. Because I love you too.'

when Robert Clark's dad died

Robert Clark loved his dad heaps. *In fact*, thought Robert, *he's probably the best dad in the world*.

So, when Robert's dad died suddenly in a car accident, Robert wanted to die too.

At the funeral, Robert couldn't stand it.

He wanted to race up to the coffin, rip off the lid and scream, 'Dad, wake up. I love you!'

Somehow, Robert thought there might still be a chance that his dad would come back. That maybe he could bring him back. His mum was always saying how useless doctors were. But what's a kid to do when the adults have given up already?

During the bit in the funeral where there's lots of talking and stuff, the minister said it was a time of great sadness but also a time for happiness. Because the memories of his dad would live on forever. Everyone had to be very strong, he said, because Rob's dad wouldn't want them being sad all the time.

So, when it came time to put the coffin in the hole, little Robert Clark took a deep breath, called on all the strength he could find in his ten-year-old body, and said, 'Goodbye, Daddy.' He tried very hard not to cry. But he did.

A long, sad, lonely time after the funeral, Robert's mum said they were going to have to live with her brother Dave. That way they'd save money and, since Dave had never married, it would give him some company, too.

Anywhere but Daggy Dave's, thought Robert.

He's such a loony.

Daggy Dave had two big problems. He never stopped talking. And he thought he was funny. But he wasn't.

His favourite way to get people laughing was to make up silly poems – rude poems, mostly – and when that didn't work, he'd play tricks like putting plastic blowflies in your breakfast or holding his throat and pretending to choke to death. **Four days in a row**.

When Rob and his mum arrived, Dave straight away told them three of the worst 'funny' poems Rob had ever heard, and then talked for three hours and ten minutes about what a hilarious day he'd had.

What would be funny, thought Robert darkly, *is if Dave really did choke to death.*

Finally, Dave showed Robert his new room. And do you know what? Rob felt guilty. Because Dave had done it up for him, just how he had it at home. All his favourite footballers were up on the wall and there was a bag of lollies on his pillow.

And something else. A present. Just about the best present a kid could ask for.

A tiny little puppy.

Robert slept as soundly that night as he had for months, with his puppy in his arms and its sweet, warm breath against his neck.

Although Robert missed his dad terribly, life with Dave wasn't as bad as Robert thought. Even though Dave never, ever shut up, and even though he told the same rotten poems a hundred times, at least it was never quiet. Robert hated quiet times because that's when he thought about his dad.

One Saturday morning, Dave said the best way to make life interesting was to start each day differently. **So he tipped his breakfast on his head.** Robert really did laugh at that one. And he even laughed at one of Dave's poems:

There once was a man
from the Rises,

Whose ears were two
different sizes.
One ear was so small
It heard nothing at all,
And the other so big it won prizes.

'While we're all sitting here having a good time,' said Dave, 'I might tell you a story.'

Oh no, thought Robert, his smile disappearing. *Here we go again.*

'Once upon a time,' began Dave, 'there was a boy called Robert Clark. And Robert Clark's dad had died.'

I don't want to hear this, thought Robert, putting his head in his hands.

'Robert and his mum went to live with

his wacky uncle,' continued Dave. 'Now, this uncle really was off the planet, except for one little thing. He knew how to enjoy himself. And knowing how to enjoy yourself means knowing all about death. It's like this, young Robert. Your dad is in heaven. I know that for sure because we all go to heaven.'

'Even you?' asked Robert, trying to be funny, but then wishing he hadn't.

'Especially me,' replied Dave. 'Someone's got to do the jokes. And I'm not talking about religion, either. I'm talking about things fitting together. Making sense. Think about rain. Rain makes things grow, and then the extra rain runs back into rivers and into the

sea. The sun heats the sea, which makes a type of steam, which makes clouds, which makes more rain. And so it goes. Perfect. In fact, everything on this earth is perfect. Except for people. People can be cruel to each other. They kill each other and they let people starve. So it makes sense that there must be another place where we're nice to each other. To make it all fit together. And that's where your dad is. Heaven.'

Rob lifted his head. 'Would he be able to get the footy on TV?' he asked.

'Of course,' said Dave. 'I don't know why some people go to heaven early, like your dad. But there must be a reason, because whoever

or whatever made us could have given us skin made out of steel if they'd wanted to.'

Rob thought about that. 'Maybe Dad went early to build a house for us,' he said.

'Perhaps,' said Dave. 'You will see your dad again, but there's no rush. I'm not scared of death – it's a good thing in a way. Can you imagine the **smell** if we all lived to a thousand?'

And for the first time since his dad had died, Robert started to feel better inside. **Really better.** Who would have guessed the reason would be one of Daggy Dave's talks? In fact, Robert even found himself wanting to spend more time with

Dave. They started going for walks every day with Sally, Rob's new puppy.

Dave made up useless poems as they walked, of course, but they really did have a laugh together watching Sally. She was a very naughty puppy. Once she did a wee on a grumpy old man's leg, and then did a huge poo on the footpath. But before Robert could pick it up, a really rude skateboarder raced past and ran right over it, and it stuck to his wheel!

Sally sniffed and chewed everything in sight. Even a parking inspector's shoe. Dave was always telling Rob how much he loved their walks, and saying, 'I wouldn't be dead

for quids,' which he explained was just a silly old saying that meant he wouldn't be dead for anything – even lots of money.

Well, life has its twists and turns. Unfortunately, it was only a year later that Dave was run over on the way home after winning lots of money at the horse races. He died instantly.

Now, you'd think that Robert would have been crushed by Dave's death. Broken-hearted. Especially after losing his dear dad only a year and a half before. But this time was different. Of course Robert missed Dave, but

he also remembered what Dave had said.

At the funeral, Robert knew Dave would want it to be a happy day, so he asked his mum if he could read a poem. 'I suppose so,' said his mum. 'But you'd better let me read it first.'

'I want it to be a surprise,' said Robert.

'Well, all right,' said his mum. 'But remember, funerals are very serious. Don't do anything that Dave wouldn't have wanted you to do.'

'I won't,' said Robert.

So at the funeral, after the talking bit, the minister asked if anyone would like to say a few words.

'Yes, I would,' said Robert.

Everyone looked around and thought, *How lovely*.

Robert walked up to the front and said quietly to the minister, 'I've written a poem but it's pretty long, so you might like to sit down.'

'Oh, thank you,' said the minister. But he wouldn't have thanked Robert if he'd known what would happen next.

Secretly, before the funeral started, Robert had put a whoopee cushion on the minister's seat. So when the minister sat down, a huge ripper went off underneath him.

Robert had seen people look red and

embarrassed before, but never as bad as this. It was one of the best blurters he'd ever heard. The poor minister obviously didn't know whether to pretend nothing had happened or check his seat – which would prove it was him – or just get up and walk out.

Robert knew Dave would be watching from heaven and absolutely loving it.

He leant into the microphone. 'This is just a short poem, really,' said Robert, 'about my Uncle Dave, who helped me very much.' Then he started to read.

Poor Daggy Dave,
He ran out of luck.
Won all this money,
Then got hit by a truck.

the girl who told lies

Jacinta Ronis told lies. All the time. Big, whopper, shameless lies. Sneaky, greasy, slimy lies. Clever, hurtful, evil lies. And got away with them **every time.**

I first realised how bad it was during a maths test at school. I was sitting right

behind Jacinta and I could see her cheating by looking across at Sylvia Benetta's answers. But Jacinta was also madly scribbling on an extra piece of paper. At first, I couldn't understand why.

After the test, our teacher, Mr Lyons, said it was clear that one of the girls had cheated because their answers were exactly the same.

'It wasn't me!' said Jacinta. 'Look, I've written down how I worked everything out.'

Mr Lyons studied her rather messy page of figures closely. 'I can't make much sense of these,' he said. 'That's not to say I don't believe you, though. Do you have any back-up work, Sylvia?'

'No,' said Sylvia. 'I suppose I found the questions pretty easy so I just wrote the answers straight down.'

'Easy because you're a filthy cheat,' yelled Jacinta.

'That's enough!' shouted Mr Lyons.

I knew Sylvia would have found the questions dead simple because she was super brainy. I'd paid her a couple of times with chocolate biscuits to help me with my homework.

But Mr Lyons was new to our school and had no idea. 'Well, Sylvia,' said Mr Lyons. 'I think that maybe we need to have a talk after school. With your parents, as well.'

Sylvia began to cry.

Which was all I needed to yell out, 'It's not fair! I saw Jacinta cheat. I know she did!'

'You're a liar, Sandra Harris!' screamed Jacinta. 'You're just jealous because my parents are together and yours have split up.'

'No, they haven't!' I yelled.

'You're such a liar,' said Jacinta, with the most evil of smiles. 'When's the last time you saw your dad?'

Now, that was just about the most awful, cruel thing anyone could say to me. Because Dad had left. A few weeks ago. He and Mum had been fighting terribly, so Dad said it was for the best that he stayed out of the way for

a while. Until things settled down.

Dad said it would all be OK, eventually. But I wasn't so sure and it made me sick. I missed him so much.

Unfortunately, Jacinta lived only two doors down from us and her mother was one of those people who knew everybody else's business. 'She's the nastiest gossip I've ever met,' my mum was always saying.

Of course, the other kids soon found out that Dad had left, which made Jacinta right and me a liar.

And after her success of fixing up both Sylvia and me in the same day, Jacinta was on a roll. No-one suspected her of lying, and the way she'd been able to make Sylvia cry in front of the class and hurt me so terribly made everyone a little bit scared of her.

So people started to suck up. Just in case she decided to go for them next. It almost made me puke watching them. Wimpy, greasy lot, they were.

'Can I sit next to you, Jacinta?'

'Want to come to my place tonight?'

'Want some of my lollies? I'm full.'

Jacinta just loved it. So she thought a couple more lies might be the go, just to make sure everyone kept it up.

She accused poor Tamsin Smith of pinch- ing money from her bag, and said to

x
81

Mr Lyons she wouldn't be surprised if the money was hidden somewhere in Tamsin's desk right now. And it was! No prizes for guessing who put it there.

And then she started a rumour that Mordy Isaacs was still wetting his bed at the age of eleven. How do you prove something like that isn't true? Drag people around to your house to feel the sheets?

Sometimes, with rumours, you just have to let them run wild for a while, until a new rumour comes along to take its place. People are always looking out for something fresh. Besides, jumping up and down too much can often make it worse.

But by now I was sick of her lies. And so was everyone else.

I was counting on Jacinta to keep thinking that she was kicking butt. In all directions. But it was time to give her a taste of her own medicine.

Soon another maths test came along and of course Jacinta plonked herself at the desk next to Sylvia, just a little too late to catch me whispering in Sylvia's ear. Naturally, Jacinta thought she could pull the old copying trick again. But this time, Sylvia got ten out of ten — and Jacinta got zero! Nothing, nought, nix.

How could this be?

'Apart from anything else, Jacinta,' said Mr Lyons, 'it now proves that you were lying last time. I will speak to you, young lady, after school. And then, of course, to your parents.'

Sylvia had fixed her up so easily, just as I had said. It had taken no time for her to write out the correct answers, with her arm blocking Jacinta's view, and then to write out another page with every answer wrong. **Der, Jacinta.**

Later at lunch, everyone was still talking about it — and Jacinta was skulking around the corner, listening to every word.

Kathy Warren said very loudly, 'Although

84

Jacinta's turned out to be a dirty rotten liar, I don't think that should stop us having the surprise birthday party for her.'

I smiled and said even louder, 'Of course. I mean, you've been planning the party for weeks.'

And so they had. Nineteen girls were going to meet at Kathy's place for the surprise party of the century. And they were betting that Jacinta knew all about the party by now. Of course with surprise parties, sometimes knowing is half the fun.

So, as planned, Kathy said to Jacinta that if she was doing nothing after school on Friday, she should come to her place to

watch a DVD.

Jacinta happily said that she'd love to. I could tell from the triumphant look on her face that she thought she was the queen of the school, once and for all.

Well, the party did turn out to be a surprise. A huge surprise – because no-one turned up!

When Jacinta knocked on Kathy's door, her mother answered and said she was terribly sorry but Kathy had totally forgotten that she had another party that night.

'At Sandra Harris's place,' said Kathy's mother. 'It's a non-liars party, whatever that means.'

Perfect for reading anywhere! Collect them all today.

Write your shopping list on a piece of dunny paper!

ww.christophermilne.com.au

ABOUT THE AUTHOR

When successful actor and screenwriter
Christopher Milne became a father, he found
himself reading books at bedtime to his two boys,
Peter and Robert. He soon ran out of stories
to read, so he started making up his own.

He quickly discovered that if he told Pete and Rob
about good boys and girls doing very good things
all the time, they were bored stupid.

But if he told them about naughty kids doing **pooey,
rotten, disgusting** things, his sons would scream for
more. 'We want more of those naughty stories!'

'OK,' Chris would reply. 'But only if you've been good
And so the **Naughty Stories for Good Boys and Girls**
were born...

For more info on Christopher Milne and his books, go to

www.ChristopherMilne.com.au